Killer Halloween Cookies

Book Two

in

Killer Cookie

Cozy Mysteries

By

Patti Benning

Author's Note: On the next page, you'll find out how to access all of my books easily, as well as locate books by best-selling author, Summer Prescott. I'd love to hear your thoughts on my books, the storylines, and anything else that you'd like to comment on – reader feedback is very important to me. Please see the following page for my publisher's contact information. If you'd like to be on her list of "folks to contact" with updates, release and sales notifications, etc...just shoot her an email and let her know. Thanks for reading!

Also…

…if you're looking for more great reads, from me and Summer, check out the Summer Prescott Publishing Book Catalog:

http://summerprescottbooks.com/book-catalog/ for some truly delicious stories.

Contact Info for Summer Prescott Publishing:

Twitter: @summerprescott1

Blog and Book Catalog: http://summerprescottbooks.com

Email: summer.prescott.cozies@gmail.com

And…look up The Summer Prescott Fan Page on Facebook – let's be friends!

If you're an author and are interested in publishing with Summer Prescott Books – please send Summer an email and she'll send you submission guidelines.

TABLE OF CONTENTS

KILLER

HALLOWEEN COOKIES

Book two in Killer Cookie Cozy Mysteries

CHAPTER ONE

L ilah Fallon hung her apron up and glanced over at her boss, Randall Price. Technically she had another fifteen minutes until her break, but she didn't think he'd mind — or notice — if she took it a bit early. Still, it was easier to ask for forgiveness than permission. She didn't quite sneak past him, but she was careful not to draw any undue attention to herself as she slipped through the door that led to the dining area.

Free from the heat and greasy smell of the kitchen, she hurried over to the table where her best friend was waiting. She had met Valerie Palmer, known to most everyone as Val, years ago, in college. They had been roommates, first in the dorm, then later renting their first apartment together. When Lilah decided that she was ready for a change of pace from the high-stress business world that her father was so in love with, Val had been the one who had come up with the idea that Lilah should move to her hometown of Vista, Alabama.

Lilah had spent the last couple of years floating from job to job as she searched for her true calling in life. She hadn't exactly made much progress on that front, but never once had she regretted her decision to move to Vista. She loved everything about the small town, and had made some of the best friends of her life there. She even enjoyed working at the diner, and owed Randall more than she could ever repay for giving her so many chances there. Still, she was always on the lookout for something new. She didn't want to spend the rest of her life working in a small town diner, no matter how much she liked it.

"Want some fries?" Val asked, pushing the basket of thick cut French fries towards her as she sat down.

"Thanks, but no. I've been eating here way too often lately. My body is craving something that hasn't been fried within an inch of its life."

"Your loss." Her friend pulled the fries back and dipped a couple into ketchup before popping them into her mouth. "How's the job hunt going?"

"Not well." Lilah sighed and slid Val's soda towards her, pulling a sip through the straw. "No one's hiring around here. I'm probably going to be at the diner for a while."

"Well, what exactly are you looking for?"

"I'm not sure. I guess just something that's a change of pace. I've been working here since the salon job went south, you know."

"Well the Granger Farm is hiring," her friend said, sliding the soda back across the table toward herself. "They're only looking for seasonal employees, though. To help with the holiday stuff."

"Ooh, we went to their haunted hayride last year, didn't we?" Lilah asked, perking up. "I loved that."

"I've gone every year since I can remember," Val said. Her face fell as she added, "The farm manager is trying to get it closed down, though. He says it's too much work."

"That's terrible. Don't the owners of the farm have a say?"

"They live in another state. Michigan, I think. From what I've heard, they don't care much what Mark — he's the manager — does as long as the farm keeps bringing in money and tourists."

"I hope he ends up deciding to keep the hayride going," Lilah said. "If I can get a job there, maybe I can convince him."

"I volunteer there every year. This late in the season, there's only a few paying positions left, but maybe you'll find something you like."

"Thanks." She beamed at her friend. "If the hours are right, I'll be able to work both jobs at once. I might actually start saving up some money. You're the best, Val."

"If you want to thank me, how about a piece of Randall's famous pumpkin pie, with extra whipped cream on top? We can split it, if you want."

"Sounds great. I'll pop on back and get an extra big slice."

Still smiling, Lilah hurried into the kitchen, her thoughts filled with visions of herself on a tractor, leading the haunted hayride. The diner was steady work, but there was something to be said for throwing caution to the wind every once in a while, and jumping feet first into something with a lot more potential for fun.

***

One of the best parts of working at the diner was how close it was to her home. It only took her a couple of minutes to cross the street and go halfway down the block to the little yellow house that she had been renting for the last two years. She had a car, but it had spent the last six months sitting in her driveway, waiting for her to scrape together enough money to replace the blown head gasket. The mechanic had told her that it would probably be more efficient to just buy a whole new car, but Lilah wasn't ready to see her old junker permanently retired just yet. If she did end up getting a job at the Granger Farm, then she might be able to put enough money aside to pay for repairs — which in turn would open up a whole new world for her. She could even get a job in the next town if she wanted to.

Feeling good about life, Lilah let herself into her colorful, cheery home and was immediately greeted by a beagle whose entire back end was wagging, and an orange tabby cat who rubbed against her ankles, purring.

"Hey, Winnie," she said, bending over to pet the dog. The cat meowed, bumping his head against her hand. "And hi there, Oscar. You two are happy to see me, aren't you? You're not going to like it very much if I start working a second job. I promise it will just be temporary, though. And I'll buy you extra treats."

At the mention of treats, Winnie's ears perked up and she ran over to the counter on which Lilah kept two cookie jars. The first one, shaped like an owl, was filled with dog and cat treats, and the second, plainer one had human cookies. Lilah was just waiting for the day that she reached into the wrong one by mistake and got a mouth full of beef flavored dog treat. It was bound to happen eventually, and she kept thinking that it might be smart to get a new system. For now, the setup worked just fine, though. She reached into the owl jar and grabbed a pair of treats, one of which she tossed to Winnie — it bounced off her nose when she tried to catch it, and she ended up chasing it across the kitchen — and the other she set on the floor for Oscar to examine. Then she reached into the human cookie jar and took out a treat for herself.

She was especially proud of these cookies, because she had made them entirely on her own. They were basic sugar cookies with homemade icing that she had colored orange for the upcoming holiday. Nothing special, but definitely tasty. She was really beginning to get the hang of this whole cookie making thing, thanks to her friend and neighbor, Margie Hatch. The older woman was a patient teacher, and always ended their cooking sessions on a good note — usually with a plate of cookies and a cold drink from her seemingly bottomless fridge.

Lilah bit into the cookie and closed her eyes. This was the life. She had her beloved pets, a delicious dessert that she had made herself, and the prospect of a new job in front of her. It was shaping up to be a great autumn.

KILLER HALLOWEEN COOKIES BOOK TWO IN KILLER COOKIE COZY MYSTERIES

CHAPTER TWO

"So I just stand here until someone comes by?"

"Right. Hold as still as you can so they don't notice you too soon, then when they get near you, sort of jump out at them. Maybe scream or moan, I don't know. If there's little kids, be less scary."

"Okay…" Lilah looked down at herself doubtfully. She was dressed as a scarecrow, and the costume was already uncomfortably warm but mostly all her shifts would be would be at night when it was cooler. When Val had said that there weren't many paying jobs left at the farm, she had been right. Still, she supposed that acting as a living prop for the hayride would be fun enough, and she couldn't complain about the check she'd be taking home at the end of every week. "That's it? That's all I have to do?"

"Pretty much. Like Mrs. Perry said, it's not a hard job, but you do have to stand around in the cornfield for a few hours, then when it gets dark head out to the trail for the hayride. Some people don't like being on their feet that long."

"I'm used to it," she said, smiling. "I work as a waitress. Thanks for showing me the ropes, Johnny."

"Not a problem. Should we give it a dry run? I'll go out to the start of the maze, and start walkin' through, and you jump out at me when I come by. I've gotta do a walk-through anyway, to make sure everything's perfect for opening night."

"All right. I'll just, uh, be standing here."

Johnny shot her a thumbs up and began walking back out of the maze. Lilah watched until he had rounded the corner, then began tugging at her costume. It was tight in all of the wrong places, and she was beginning to get the feeling that it hadn't been made for a woman's form. The burlap mask — really just a sack with eye and mouth holes cut out — was uncomfortable too, scratchy and stiff. Still, she was glad that she had gotten the job. It should be a lot more fun once the corn maze and hayride opened and she had actual guests to spook. She had heard that there would be fog machines this year, along with the creepy music and masked menaces. She half wished that she could be *on* the ride, instead of being part of it.

Her staff radio crackled at her hip. She fumbled with the costume, trying to reach it. At last she pulled it off of her waistband and hit the transmit button.

"Hello? Sorry — I missed that. Could you repeat it?"

"Yeah, it's Johnny. I'm not going to be able to do that walk-through after all. The boss wants me for something else. You just go on and head home. Keep the costume clean. See ya' opening night."

"Right. Okay. Thanks again for showing me everything."

She released the button and waited a few seconds in case he was going to reply, then clipped the walkie talkie back onto her pants.

Going home early wasn't a bad thing; she could practice her scary shrieks in the mirror just as well as she could here, and she would be able to get out of the uncomfortable costume sooner.

Lilah turned right and began walking back the direction that she and Johnny had come when he was showing her her spot in the maze. It wasn't until she came to the first T that she realized she hadn't been paying all that much attention on the way in. Which way had they come? From the left? She looked down both paths, but couldn't see anything familiar along either.

"Left it is, then," she muttered. Even if she was wrong, it couldn't take her *that* long to find her way out of the maze… could it?

Nearly an hour later, she had her answer. It most definitely *could* take her a painfully long time to find her way out of the maze. The thought had crossed her mind to page Johnny and ask him for help, but it was just too embarrassing. She didn't want to admit to *anyone* that she had spent the last hour getting more and more lost in a corn maze. She was beginning to get tired of walking, not to mention the fact that it was sweltering inside the costume, and she was pretty sure that she was getting a rash from the burlap. Why did she think working on a farm would be a good idea? What if she got lost like

23

this when the maze was open? Well, at least then she would be able to follow the other families out.

"Okay, I'm pretty sure I've been here before," she said, stopping at a three-way split in the path. "I think I took both sides, so maybe the middle one this time."

Crossing her fingers, she continued on straight, and was rewarded a few minutes later when she rounded a corner and saw the corn maze's exit. She hurried towards it, eager to get to Margie's car — her friend had been kind enough to let her borrow it for the evenings while she worked this temporary job — and store the terribly uncomfortable outfit in her trunk. She was only feet away from freedom when the sound of raised voices made her jerk to a halt.

"Your flyers still advertise the hayride. I don't know if I want to put money down on something that's still in use."

"Look, we're gonna use it for a day or two before the ride's shut down, then it's yours. Nothing's gonna happen to it. If you don't want to put a down payment on it, that's fine, but I'm going to keep going down the list of other buyers. I'm not holding it without anything down."

She didn't recognize the first speaker's voice, but she definitely recognized the second. It was Mark Perry, the farm manager. He had been there at her job interview. Lilah took a couple of steps backwards and hid around the corner. This didn't sound like a conversation she should interrupt.

"Fine. Here's two-hundred, but I expect it back if the trailer's broken or damaged in anyway. It better be in exactly the same condition that it is now. I'm not paying for junk."

"You'll get your money back if anything happens," said Mark. "But it's not going to. Is that it? Do you want to look at anything else?"

"I guess I'll take a look at those fog machines, too. Might as well, since I'm here."

The two men's voices began to fade as they walked away. Lilah waited until she couldn't hear them anymore, then cautiously approached the exit and poked her head out, looking in both directions to make sure the coast was clear. What had she just heard? It sounded like the farm manager was a bit closer to shutting down the haunted hayride for good than Val seemed to think. She knew that she would have to call her friend right away when she got home. It might be too late, since money had already traded hands, but maybe there was still something they could do.

Before heading to her car, Lilah decided to swing by the farm store and see if they had anything cold to drink. After spending an hour wandering around the maze in full costume, she was parched. She straightened her costume , then pushed through the door. She recognized the woman at the counter immediately; it was Mrs. Perry, a kind-faced woman who Lilah would have guessed was in her fifties.

"Hi, dear," she said after a moment's silence as she looked the living scarecrow that had just walked into her store. "You're the new hire, aren't you?"

Lilah nodded. "Yeah. Sorry, I was just —"

"Don't apologize, I think it's a fine idea to get used to your costume before the big day. We've had people stumble over their own feet on opening night too many times to count. You're a friend of Val's, right?"

"That's right."

"She's been such a blessing around the farm. She's been volunteering here for years, you know? Never asks for a penny. I'd wager she loves this place almost as much as I do, and that's saying something. A friend of hers is a friend of mine. I'm so glad we could help you out."

"Oh, um, thank you. When she mentioned this job, I just knew I had to have it. I came to the haunted hayride last year, and it was amazing." Realizing that maybe the hayride wasn't the best subject, since it was closing down soon, she cleared her throat and got to the point. "I was actually wondering if you sell anything cold to drink here?"

"We sure do. How does a nice cup of cold apple cider sound?"

"Wonderful," Lilah said, reaching into her pocket for a five-dollar bill that she was pretty certain had gone through the wash with her pants the other day.

"No need to pay," Mrs. Perry said with a wave of her hand. "Employees get cider and donuts for free. Come, follow me, I'll show you where the staff fridge is."

A few minutes later, Lilah was on her way out the door with a Styrofoam cup of apple cider and a freshly made cinnamon donut in her hand. She liked Mrs. Perry already; it was a shame that this was only a seasonal job. If she could work here year-round, she'd be happy.

"Whoops, sorry," she said as the door to the little farm shop swung open right in front of her. She nearly ran into the person that was walking through. "Reid?"

"Lilah? What are you doing here? What are you wearing?" The tall, dark, and handsome businessman looked bewildered, and Lilah realized that she was still in the scarecrow get-up.

"I work here now," she said. "Val got me the job."

"Ah," he said, as if that explained everything. "Well, it's nice to see you. We'll talk later. You're spilling your cider."

With that, he pushed past her and into the shop. Lilah jerked her cup back upright and stared after him. What was *he* doing here? He had a clipboard in his left hand, but she couldn't see what was on it. Whatever it was, it must have been important. Reid never brushed her off like that.

The door swung shut in front of her face, and with a mental shrug, Lilah decided that finding out what he was doing could wait for later. Right now, she had cider and a donut to enjoy, and a scratchy, too-tight scarecrow outfit to take off. She could only worry about so many things at once, and there was no reason to add Reid to that list. She had never been interested in his doings before; why should she start now?

CHAPTER THREE

Margie's kitchen was hot and smelled of vanilla. Neither was unexpected; the older woman was almost always cooking *something,* and as a result her kitchen was always a good ten to twenty degrees warmer than the rest of her house. Lilah, who was used to working around food and hot stoves all day, much preferred the sweet scent of vanilla extract to the cloying grease smell that seemed to stick with her after every shift at the diner.

"Keep beating those egg whites. They aren't quite ready yet," Margie said as she peered into the bowl. "You're nearly there."

Lilah tightened her grip on the electric mixer and watched the mixture of egg, cream of tartar, and salt as it whipped into a froth.

She still wasn't sure how it was possible to make cookies without any flour, but she had complete faith in her friend's baking skills. If Margie thought it would work, then it would work.

"That's it," the older woman said at last. "Keep beating them, and I'll add the sugar."

Gradually the mixture started to form stiff peaks and became silkier looking. Once all of the sugar that they had measured out beforehand had been added in, Lilah turned the mixer off and helped her friend separate the batch into two bowls. The first, they folded vanilla extract into, and the second got lemon zest. Then they split the vanilla mixture into a few more bowls, and added drops of food coloring to each. They spooned the mixtures into piping bags, and Margie began showing her how to make shapes on the parchment paper lined baking trays.

"The ghosts are lemon-flavored," she said. "Use the green for the witches, the red for the devils, and the orange and yellow mixtures can be alternated to look like candy corn. Take your time, but the shapes don't have to be perfect. Even lumpy ghosts will taste great."

"I've never been a great artist, but I'll do what I can," Lilah said. "I can't wait to try them. I've never had meringues before. Not meringue cookies, anyway. I love lemon meringue pies."

"Meringue is what this sweetened egg mixture is called. It can be used in quite a few different desserts. Now that you know how to make it, you should try experimenting with it. It's pretty versatile — you can do fruit flavors, vanilla, of course, peppermint, chocolate... the list goes on."

"The ingredients are pretty simple, too," Lilah said. "Meringue cookies sound so fancy, but they only need eggs and sugar and flavoring."

Her friend nodded. "See? Baking isn't really that difficult, once you know what you're doing. Even the things that sound intimidating are usually pretty simple. Have you made anything on your own yet?"

"I made some sugar cookies with icing a few days ago. I meant to bring them over, but, erm... I ate them all. I'll make you some next time."

"I can't wait to try them. I'm so glad you've begun baking on your own, Lilah. It's good for the soul.

The two of them worked in silence after that, drawing ghosts, devils, witches, and candy corn on the baking sheets. Once all four sheets were in the oven, the two women were able to take a breather. They sat down at the kitchen table, which was cluttered with Halloween decorations waiting to be put up, and Margie poured them a couple of glasses of iced tea.

"How are things going with you?" Lilah asked as she took a sip of her tea.

"Oh, fine. I've been busier than ever, but have been enjoying every second of it. I'll be volunteering at the hayride's opening night again, so I'll probably see you there. I'm a bit behind on putting up my own decorations, because I've spent the last few days helping the library get ready for their 'Spook-tastic Campfire Stories' event. Oh, and I've got some family coming in a few weeks."

"That sounds nice. Who?"

"My son, and his wife and three children. They'll be staying with me for a few days before continuing on to visit her family up in New York."

"That sounds like a full house," Lilah said. "And I thought I had it bad when my mom came to stay that week my dad was in Germany."

"Oh, it will be nice. I don't get to see them very often and it's been a long time since I've had little ones running around. I'm hoping that they'll stop by on their way back through, even if just for a night. They live in Texas. Have I told you that? Right on the border of Texas and Louisiana, in fact."

She knew that Margie had two children, a son and a daughter, but she hadn't ever heard many details about them. Her friend rarely talked about her past, though Lilah had been able to gather that Mr. Hatch had passed away far too soon, and there had been sort of falling out with her daughter. It would be interesting to meet at least the one part of her family; maybe her son would be able to shed more light on Margie's past.

"They're driving from Texas to New York? That's a long trip, especially with kids," Lilah said. She didn't have very much experience with children herself, but imagined that they wouldn't much enjoy spending hour after hour in the car.

"They don't know what they're in for," the older woman agreed with a chuckle. "Anyway, enough about me. How did your first day at the farm go?"

"It was just training. It went... okay." She wasn't eager to bring up the fact that she had gotten lost in the corn maze. She tried to come up with something else to say. "Oh, I saw Reid there. I don't know what he was doing — he was carrying a clipboard and seemed pretty distracted."

"He must have been collecting petitions," Margie said, nodding sagely.

Lilah raised her eyebrows. "Petitions?"

"A couple of us have been going around town and collecting signatures to keep the haunted hayride open. We figure if we get enough people and we send it to the owners, they'll have to tell Mark Perry he can't shut it down. We just have to show them how popular it is.

"That's a great idea. Can I help?"

"Of course. Do you think you could collect any signatures while you're there before or after your shift?"

"I can do that." She sighed. "I really hope that the ride stays open." Lilah considered telling Margie about the conversation between Mark and that man while she was in the corn maze, but decided against it. There was no reason to worry her friend; it was possible that they might still be able to make a difference and keep the haunted hayride open.

CHAPTER FOUR

"Welcome to Granger Farm. The corn maze opens in half an hour, and the haunted hayride will begin at seven o'clock. The farm shop is selling fresh apple cider and donuts, along with candy apples, homemade kettle corn, and hot dogs. Here's a flyer. I hope you enjoy your visit."

Lilah handed the family a pamphlet with a smile, and put their five-dollar entrance fee in the pouch she was wearing at her waist. It was the very first day that the Halloween attraction was open to the public this year, and already the parking area was getting crowded. It was easy to let the upbeat and excited mood of most of the guests sweep her away. She was even eager to begin working in the corn maze as a living prop, even though it meant getting back into that uncomfortable, itchy costume. She felt a bit bad that she hadn't managed to gather any signatures for the petition to keep the hayride open yet, but she had been corralled into working at the entrance as soon as she arrived, due to one of the high school kids that was supposed to do it not showing up. She figured she would have enough time to get at least a few signatures during her break, between her time in the corn maze and working at the hayride.

"Welcome to Granger Farm… Oh, hi, Val."

"Hey. I'm just here to help with the kiddie maze. I saw you, and thought I'd stop by to see how you're doing."

"I'm doing well," Lilah told her friend. "I think I'm really going to enjoy this job. Thanks so much for telling me about it."

"Not a problem. I thought you might enjoy it." Val grinned. "And hey, since it's just a temporary job, I bet your curse won't apply."

"My curse?"

"Sweetie, you haven't been able to keep a job for more than a few weeks ever since you left your father's company — other than working at the diner, of course. After seeing what happened at the salon, I'm pretty sure you must have rubbed a genie's bottle the wrong way, or maybe broken a bunch of mirrors in a past life."

"Thanks a lot," Lilah said, rolling her eyes. "I'm cursed. That's great to hear."

"Oh, I'm sure you'll find your perfect job eventually." Her friend patted her on the arm. "Anyway, I've got to go herd a flock of fourth graders through the kids' maze. I'll come find you during your break. Good luck."

With that, Val left. Lilah shook her head and tried to focus on greeting the next family, but she couldn't get the other woman's words out of her head. Was she really cursed? It was true that she hadn't been able to hold any job other than waitressing at the diner for more than a couple of weeks. Hopefully this job at the farm would mark a turning point for her. She really needed the money, and she was determined not to mess it up.

An hour later, Lilah was standing at her spot in the corn maze sweating into her costume. It was a semi-cool day at around seventy degrees, but with the sun beating down on her and her entire body covered in burlap, it was uncomfortable. Even so, she was having fun. A couple of people had come by already, and she had successfully startled them. She had perfected the art of standing perfectly still with her head drooping down until her next victim walked by. Most people didn't realize that she was a living person until it was too late, and would jump back with a yelp when she moved.

As far as jobs went, this was definitely one of the more entertaining ones that she had ever had. It would be hard to beat getting paid to scare people, though what she was really looking forward to was the hayride. The haunted hayride took place after dark, and the path that the tractor took through the cornfield and the orchard would be lined with fog machines. It should be much cooler, for one thing, and she wouldn't have to stand in one spot the entire time.

"Grarr!" she exclaimed, jumping towards a young couple that was passing her by. The girl let out a scream and stumbled backwards, then burst out laughing at her own reaction. Her boyfriend chuckled, and looked Lilah up and down.

"Great costume, dude," he said.

She snorted and returned to her post. Dude. Maybe she should ask for a more flattering costume. Still, a compliment *was* a compliment. Apparently she made a very good scarecrow.

Lilah heard voices and immediately got back into her pose. She slitted her eyes, waiting for her next victim to appear. She wasn't prepared to see Reid round the corner, followed by a girl who looked to be about twelve, and a boy who was four or five. The girl trailed behind, her eyes on her cell phone, and the boy was eagerly exploring every inch of the path. When he saw her, he rushed right up close and stared at her.

Not wanting to scare the kids too much, Lilah moved her head slowly until she was looking down at the boy. "Boo," she said.

"Boo!" he yelled right back at her, and, giggling, ran to hide behind Reid, who gave a half smile at the sight of her in the scarecrow costume.

Straightening up, she stepped away from the pole and began walking towards them with slow, staggering steps. The boy squealed, enjoying every second of it, and ran away from her. The girl startled and jumped back, looking up from her phone for the first time to see a scarecrow staggering towards her. Reid laughed.

"That's why you shouldn't have your nose in your phone all the time, Alisha," he said.

"I just got it for my birthday, Uncle Reid," she replied. "I still need to finish downloading all the apps my friends have." But she put the phone in her pocket anyway and rushed ahead to join her brother, letting out a yelp of her own as the scarecrow reached towards her. Reid shot a smile towards Lilah as he followed them, and she couldn't help but smile back. She hadn't known that he had his niece and nephew in town, and she thought it was nice of him to take them to the farm for the day. She wouldn't have guessed that the busy, business-oriented man would be good with children, too. It just went to show that people were full of surprises, she thought.

She got a forty-five-minute break starting at six between her shifts in the corn maze and at the haunted hayride. After taking a few minutes to refresh herself with a cup of cold cider and a couple of donuts, Lilah hurried back to Margie's car and got out of her costume, then got out the clipboard with the petition on it that Margie had given her to collect signatures to keep the haunted hayride open. She wandered around the farm, enjoying the sights and autumn smells, and the soft breeze that did wonders to cool her down now that she wasn't wearing the costume over her clothes. She stopped a few people and asked them to sign before moving on to a new area — she didn't want to bother anyone too much; they were all here to enjoy the farm, after all. After a good half-hour of this, she had twenty signatures, and felt quite pleased with herself as she went to get changed back into her costume for the haunted hayride.

Chasing the tractor through the foggy corn field and orchard was just as fun as Lilah had hoped. She was the only scarecrow, but other employees were dressed as witches, werewolves, mummies, and zombies. Someone dressed as a vampire lay in the coffin along the side of the path, and a couple of women in pale dresses and carrying flickering lights followed the hayride at a distance as ghosts. Speakers set up intermittently along the path played eerie sounds — howls and wails and moans. The guests seemed to thoroughly enjoy themselves, and by the time her shift was over, Lilah could hardly believe that Mark Perry wanted to shut the hayride down. How could anyone want to get rid of such a popular attraction? She could only hope that between her, Reid, Val, and Margie, they would get enough signatures to convince the farm owners to force Mark to keep the hayride running.

CHAPTER FIVE

T he next few days were busier than ever. Working two jobs was hard; Lilah only got about an hour off between her morning shift at the diner, and her evening at the farm. She felt bad leaving Oscar and Winnie alone for such a long time, but she reminded herself — and them — that it was only temporary. It helped that Margie had offered to check in on them around dinnertime every evening. Lilah knew she owed her neighbor a serious favor, but wasn't sure yet how she would repay it.

Saturday afternoon, she was even more wiped out than usual when she got home from the diner. It had been an exhausting week, and she was looking forward to the next day, her one day off of both jobs. The decision to leave her fast-paced yet financially comfortable job at her father's firm was something that she sometimes doubted on days like today. It was one thing to leave a job that she found mind-numbingly boring if she was following her passion, as had been her original plan, but right now she was feeling like she wasn't even achieving that. Sure, she was working two jobs that she enjoyed, but neither were long term careers, and neither were something she would want to spend the rest of her life doing. There had to be *something* out there that was both interesting and would make for a lucrative career. Something that she could see herself caring about. Something where she would actually be making a difference in people's day-to-day lives.

Trying to shake off the feeling of melancholy and ignore the fact that she hadn't actually *achieved* anything worth noting so far during her life, Lilah poured herself a glass of cold water from the pitcher in the fridge and went to sit on the porch to enjoy a few minutes of sunlight while Winnie sniffed around the yard. The beagle was beginning to look a bit porky around the ribs, and Lilah had the sneaking suspicion that that was due to the fact that she had been replacing walks with treats more often than not lately. Both she and the dog could use a good jog — but that would have to wait until tomorrow. It was time for her to head out to the Granger Farm and scare the pants off of a few guests.

"Hey, Johnny," she said as she walked past the milking barn, her mask under her arm. "How's it going?"

"Not bad at all, Ms. Fallon," he said. "It's a right busy day, and we've got a large group coming tonight for the maze and hayride."

"Sounds like fun," Lilah said. "And you can just call me Lilah. It doesn't make sense for me to call you by your first name and you to be all formal and call me Ms. Fallon."

"Sorry, ma'am," he said sheepishly. "It's habit. I'll try and remember to call you Lilah from now on."

She continued on her way, feeling lighthearted and happy. So far all of the other employees at the farm had been nice to her, and she hadn't made a single major mistake. The guests had all been great too, other than one kid who had tried to poke her with a stick. They *wanted* to be scared, which made her job pretty easy.

Back at her usual spot in the corn maze, Lilah pulled on her mask and got to work. The time passed a lot more quickly than it had the first day; she hardly even noticed the discomfort of the outfit anymore, and she had gotten better at judging when the next group of maze goers would appear; should could tell by the screams from around the corner just before her, where a man dressed as a werewolf lurked.

After a pretty successful shift in the corn maze — she had startled one woman so much that she had dropped her cup of apple cider, which Lilah felt a bit bad about — she pulled off her mask and headed back to the little farm store for her own cup of cider and a donut. The shop was busier than normal, so she took her snack outside and sat on one of the benches in the shade to relax.

"Hey, scarecrow." Lilah looked up to see Reid standing a few feet away, smiling. She quickly swallowed her mouthful of donut.

"Reid," she said. "Hi. Are you here with your niece and nephew again?"

"Not today. Mrs. Perry actually asked me to stop by. She gave me some good news, and a dozen free donuts. Do you want one?"

Lilah considered the proffered bag, then shook her head. "I shouldn't," she said, nodding towards her own half-eaten donut. "Between these and all of the cookies I got from Margie, I've been eating way too much sugar lately. What was the good news?"

"We did it." His smiled broadened. "All of the signatures that you, Val, Margie and I got over the last few days worked. Val emailed the list to the owners of the farm yesterday, and got their reply today. They called the Perry's this morning and specifically requested that they keep the haunted hayride running."

"Awesome." Lilah grinned back at him. She usually avoided any unnecessary interactions with Reid, who had asked her out in the past only for her to turn him down, but this small victory was definitely a good time to make an exception to her usual rule of staying far away from the attractive man who lived and breathed the fast paced life that she had recently gotten out of. "You know what, maybe I will have a second donut. It's not every day that we have a cause to celebrate."

He offered her the bag again and she picked a donut out. He grabbed one himself and sat down next to her. Lilah was suddenly self-conscious of the fact that she was wearing an unflattering scarecrow costume. She immediately admonished herself for caring. Yes, Reid was attractive, there was no denying that. But he wouldn't be good for her. He was another tie to the fast-paced, ruthless business world that she was trying to avoid. He was obsessed with his work, was a slave to his phone, and traveled for work more often than was healthy; a corporate man through and through. If she was going to enter into a serious relationship with someone, she wanted it to be with someone who shared her own goals in life. She wanted a job that she loved, a cozy home that she adored, and maybe even kids if she managed to find a husband before her biological clock ran out. None of that included a man who was already married to his work.

"Are you on break, or done with work for the day?" he asked.

"Just on break," she told him. She thought she saw his face fall.

"Ah, okay. Are you going back to the corn maze?"

"The hayride," she said. "The corn maze closes after dark. I guess they've had too many issues with kids getting away from their parents in the dark. I think Johnny — one of the guys who works at

51

the farm year-round — said that next year they're going to buy some lights to line the paths with."

"That sounds like a good idea. What —" He broke off as a pair of men came out of the farm shop, bursting through the doors and shoving a woman out of the way. One of the men was red in the face, his hands clenched into fists. The other was Mark Perry, the farm manager.

"I knew something like this would happen, but *you* convinced me to put a payment down on that trailer. You better have my money, Mark, or this is going to get ugly."

"Calm down, Don. I'll get you your money. I'm not trying to cheat anyone. It's not my fault that —" Mark's gaze slipped over to Lilah and Reid, and he stopped mid-sentence. With a nod of his head, he indicated that Don should follow him, and they disappeared around the side of the building.

Lilah exchanged a look with Reid. What on earth had they just witnessed? The handsome businessman raised an eyebrow.

"Are you as curious about that as I am?" he asked. She nodded. They got up and tiptoed to the corner of the building. She was surprised at his sense of adventure, but then again, he did seem to care about the farm. He had probably been going there most of his life, after all. Reid put a finger to his lips, and they listened in silence to the hushed conversation taking place around the corner.

"— have your money by next week. I just don't have it on me."

"I need it now, Perry. If you're taking your stuff off the market, I need to look elsewhere. I put a lot down on those fog machines. If you don't give me that cash back, I'm going to view it as theft. You're running a shady operation here, trying to sell stuff that isn't even yours."

"Look, I didn't think the farm owners would care. They aren't even in this state. I guess a few people got word that I was going to shut the hayride down and collected signatures to try to show the owners that it was still a popular attraction. I just got the email from them this morning. I wasn't trying to pull anything over on you. Just give me a few days, and I'll have your deposit back to you."

"I want it tomorrow."

"Tomorrow's Sunday. The banks are closed."

"Monday, then," Don snarled. "No later than that. And I am *not* happy about any of this."

They stumbled back as the man came around the corner, but he didn't even seem to notice them. His face was still beet red, and he muttered to himself as he walked away.

"It sounds like someone's not too happy about our success," Reid said darkly.

"Yeah. But it's his own fault for trying to sell something that wasn't his in the first place." Lilah's phone buzzed in her pocket and she looked at it. "Oh crap," she said. "That's my alarm. My break's over. I've got to go."

She downed the rest of her cider in one gulp and, eating the donut as she jogged, hurried away, her mind full of questions about the conversation that she and Reid had just overheard.

CHAPTER SIX

S till shaken, Lilah was almost late to her spot along the path of the hayride. She yanked the burlap mask over her face and rushed into the orchard. The fog machines were already turned on, and with dusk fast approaching, the effect was very eerie. It didn't help that she knew that the other employees were probably all at their own stations already, and were watching her as she ran past. The mummies, especially, gave her the heebie-jeebies. With their faces covered, it was impossible to tell who they were. She was pretty sure that one of the mummies had waved at her earlier, but she hadn't the slightest idea who was underneath the wrapping.

Lilah got to her spot in the nick of time, and receded into the shadows of a gnarled apple tree just as the hayride came around the corner for the first time that night. The tractor chugged along slowly, and the group of people — adults and children alike — chattered and laughed excitedly in the trailer. It suddenly hit her what she and her friends had accomplished. Thanks to them, this haunted hayride would be around for years to come, and hundreds of people would get to enjoy it. Lilah hadn't grown up in Vista, so she didn't have quite the same attachment to the festivities at the Granger Farm that people like Val and Reid did, but she was still proud that she'd had a hand in saving one of the town's best attractions.

She staggered out of her spot behind the apple tree, her arms out to the sides and hands flopping, trying her best to look as much like an uprooted scarecrow as she could. A few of the younger children let out yelps and screams as she got nearer. The fog swirling around them made for a good effect, especially in the moonlight. It was the perfect night, not too chilly, but not as clammy and warm as some of the nights had been, with a not-quite-full moon that illuminated the path, but created dark shadows between the trees.

The people in the trailer screamed and laughed as she approached. As the trailer slowly rattled past, she retreated back into the trees to wait for the next load of spooked guests. One of the werewolves howled, a pretty convincing sound as far as she was concerned, though she had never actually heard a wolf howl in real life. To her right, the pair of mummies moaned and groaned as they stepped out of the fog, arms raised straight out in front of them. Beneath her mask, Lilah grinned. This was fun.

The next trailer trundled by a few minutes later, and she came out of hiding once more, this time running at the trailer for the last few steps. As it passed, she began walking back to her spot, when she noticed that the fog in her area seemed to be thinner than usual. She frowned and cocked her head, listening. The fog machine wasn't very loud, but it did make a noise that she had gotten used to blocking out, though she could usually hear it if she concentrated. Now, however, it was silent. Lilah glanced to her right, but there was no sign of the next trailer. She wasn't really supposed to leave her position, but if the fog machine was broken, she was sure someone would want to know.

She dashed across the path and into the thicker woods that bordered the orchard, where the fog machine was hidden. A red light was blinking on the back; it needed a refill. With a sigh, she returned to her spot in the apple trees and fished the walkie-talkie out of her costume.

"Fog machine number eight is down," she said into the device, keeping her voice low.

"Copy that. On my way." The reply was garbled, but she was pretty sure the one who answered had been Mark. She wondered fleetingly if he was still in a bad mood from his argument earlier, then pushed that thought out of her mind as she caught sight of the next tractor. She had a job to do.

By the time the tractor and trailer had passed and she was back behind the gnarled apple tree that she considered home base, the fog in her area had completely dissipated. She was about to call on her radio again when she saw movement in the trees. She recognized Mark; he was crouched over the bush that hid the fog machine and was fiddling with something. The werewolf to her right howled; her signal that another trailer was on its way. Was Mark going to be finished refilling the fog machine in time? She hoped so; he was easily visible from the path.

She peered to the right, then glanced across the way at Mark, gauging how much time he had left. Not much, she figured. Maybe half a minute. She bit her lip, watching him struggle with the fog machine. Should she offer to help? Just as she was about to leave her hiding spot behind the apple tree, she noticed a white form hurrying towards Mark from the left. It was one of the mummies; they must have noticed the fog machine was out, too.

The mummy paused to pull a prop up from the ground — a *Beware* sign that had a cruel looking stake on the other end. A frown creased Lilah's brow. They weren't supposed to mess with the props while the attraction was open, so what was this mummy doing?

She realized seconds before it happened that something was going really, really wrong. As the mummy approached Mark with the stake held up, she opened her mouth to call out a warning. The words got stuck in her throat; she felt like she was in a bad dream.

Mark looked up just as the Mummy brought the stake down. The pointed wood pierced his chest and the farm manager grunted, falling to his knees. Lilah gasped and staggered forward, not quite sure what she was going to do, but certain that she had to do *something.* At that moment, the tractor rounded the corner and chugged slowly along the path in front of her. Lilah faintly heard the people on the trailer muttering, but was too much in shock to focus on what they were saying.

She took a few weak steps towards the trailer, and as soon as it had passed hurried the rest of the way across the road, pausing only to pick up a large branch. The mummy was still there, now kneeling next to Mark, trying to hold him up.

"Get away from him!" Lilah shouted, suddenly finding her voice again as she raised the heavy branch as threateningly as she could.

"Wait! Lilah, it's me."

She recognized the voice instantly, and took a horrified step backwards, letting the branch droop even as the mummy pulled her mask off.

"Val?"

Her friend's face was pale in the moonlight, and the front of her mummy costume was stained with Mark's blood. The man wasn't moving, his eyes unblinkingly open as they stared past her.

"Val," Lilah said again, her voice shaking. She felt as if all of the strength had gone out of her. The branch fell to the ground with a thump. "Did you… did you kill him?"

"What?" her friend gasped. "No. That was the other mummy. He ran away just as the tractor was passing by. I didn't realize what he was going to do, I thought he was going to go help Mark. I swear, if I had known…" She trailed off, her eyes wide as she looked helplessly up at Lilah.

"Oh." Lilah hesitated for a moment. Her gut said to believe her friend. After all, there *had* been a few seconds when Mark and the mummy that had killed him were blocked from her view. But where had that mummy disappeared to so quickly? No, she couldn't think like that. Val wouldn't hurt a fly. "Is he…" She trailed off; the answer to her question was obvious. There was no way that Mark was alive. "We need to call the police," she said instead. "And we need to stop the hayride." Her brain felt scattered, but she knew one thing; she didn't want the kids on the next trailer to have to see any of this.

CHAPTER SEVEN

"Just calm down, ma'am, please," Officer Eldridge said, sounding exasperated. "Listen, the two of you were the only witnesses. I need to take your statements before you leave."

"I can't do this right now," Val said, her voice rising as she edged towards hysteria. She had pulled the mummy wrapping off her face, but was still wearing the rest of her costume. "I have blood on me. The blood of a dead man. Oh my goodness, I can't believe I saw someone get killed!"

She drew in a tremulous breath, and Lilah was concerned that she was going to start sobbing. She had never seen her friend this upset, though she couldn't blame her for being on the verge of a breakdown. She had just witnessed someone get brutally stabbed right in front of her, and had held his body as he died. With a chill, Lilah realized that if the killer was the other mummy, then that meant that Val must have been standing next to him or her all evening.

"I can start with the scarecrow while you compose yourself," the officer said. "Jenson, get this woman a blanket and something warm to drink, and do what you can to help her calm down."

"Yes, sir," said a young female officer, who corralled Val and lead her over to a straw bale to sit on. Officer Eldridge turned to Lilah.

"Please, tell me exactly what you saw, ma'am," he said. "Leave nothing out."

She told him about the attack, explaining how she had seen the mummy run alongside the path out of the corner of her eye, pick up a prop, and stab Mark through the chest with it. When she got to the part about the tractor rolling past, he began to look skeptical.

"You didn't actually see a second person dressed as a mummy?" She shook her head. "So what you *saw* was one person dressed as a mummy attack Mr. Perry, and a few seconds after that, the trailer passed, and there was still only one mummy, now kneeling by Mr. Perry?"

Lilah nodded slowly. She knew where he was going with this. There was no proof that there had been two mummies. And if there had only been one person dressed as a mummy near Mark Perry when he was killed, and that person was Val... that would make Val the killer.

"I see." Eldridge glanced over his shoulder at where the hysterical woman in half a mummy costume was huddled in a blanket. "Was Mr. Perry alive when you approached them?"

"No," Lilah said, feeling slightly sick as she said it. No, he was already gone. How could it take only seconds for a living person to become a dead body? It seemed impossible, but it was all-too real.

"Did you touch the body, or anything in the immediate area?"

"No. Well, I might have touched the fog machine a few minutes before, I don't remember. And I dropped a stick."

"Who reported the broken fog machine?"

"I did," she said, the sick feeling growing stronger. "If I hadn't called it in, then Mark wouldn't have come out to refill it. And he'd still be alive."

"Did you see anyone interfere with the fog machine earlier this evening?"

"No."

It went on like that for a few minutes more, him questioning her about seemingly small things, and her answering as best she could while her mind wandered between thoughts of Val, and wondering what she could have done differently. She had frozen when she saw the mummy attack. Yet another reason his death was all her fault; if she had managed to get a warning out, he might have been able to defend himself. She had let a man die through inaction. As far as she was concerned, that was almost as bad as if she had killed him herself.

She waited for Val after that, not wanting to leave without saying something to her friend, making sure she was okay. No one had told her that she had to leave, so she hung around the periphery, watching what seemed like the entire Vista police department spread out through the woods in search of the second mummy. Val's questioning seemed to take a lot longer than hers, and she was beginning to get concerned that her friend was going to be arrested on the spot. In fact, she was certain that Officer Eldridge was reaching for his handcuffs just as a call came in on the police radios. She was close enough to Officer Jenson, the woman that had fetched a blanket for Val, to hear what was said.

"We found a costume in the woods. Looks like it was supposed to be a mummy. Possible bloodstains on one arm. No sign of the perp."

Lilah felt a rush of relief. She tried to tell herself it was just because she was glad that her friend was free, but couldn't deny that a small part of her had suspected that the killer could have been Val. Not because she thought her friend was a killer, but because Eldridge was right; she had never actually seen a second mummy approach Mark.

The officer nodded to Val, and the woman left hurriedly, heading directly towards Lilah. She wrapped her arms around her friend, then pulled back.

"This is so horrible," Val said. "I can't even process it right now. I feel like I'm sleepwalking. Who could have done something like this?"

"Don't you know who was in the other mummy costume?" Lilah asked. "I'm sure the police will be able to find them."

"That's the thing… I have no idea who it was. The people who normally play the mummies are an older married couple, and they both called in sick tonight. Mark had to scurry to find replacements. I offered to do it, but the other mummy got here late, and we didn't talk at all since the event had already opened. It could have been anyone. All I know is it was someone a little bit taller than me. I honestly couldn't even tell you if it was a man or a woman. I was too focused on the job to notice."

"That's scary," Lilah said with a shudder. "It could literally have been anyone. Do you know if anyone around the farm had an issue with Mark?" Even as she said the words, she realized that she knew someone who had been very angry with the farm manager just a few hours before; Don, the person who had been planning to buy some of the equipment from the haunted hayride.

"I don't know," her friend said. "I don't even want to think about it right now. I'm sure I'll be okay to talk about all of this later, but right now I just want to go home and take a long shower. I think some of his blood soaked through my shirt. I can feel it on my skin, Lilah."

"You shouldn't be driving, Val. I'll take you home in Margie's car. We can get yours tomorrow." Lilah was shaken, too, but her friend was the one who had held the man during his last breaths. She couldn't even imagine what that had been like.

Her friend nodded and the two women walked away from the flashing lights of the police cars, both of them full of guilt at the thought that they had been witness to a murder — and had done nothing to stop it.

CHAPTER EIGHT

"Thanks for coming over on such short notice, dear. I wouldn't have asked, but I'm just in such a crunch to get these cookies made for the library's next book sale. Mary-Lou was supposed to bring the snacks this time, but she's ill. I probably shouldn't have volunteered, but I know how much everyone enjoys fresh treats during the sale. It's such a long day for all of the volunteers."

"Don't worry about it, Margie," Lilah said as she walked into her friend's house. "The farm is still shut down while the police comb the property for evidence, so I don't have anything else to do tonight. I'm more than happy to spend the evening helping you bake cookies. I enjoy it."

"Oh, that's so nice of you to say. I promise you won't leave empty-handed. I always make extra, so you should be able to take plenty home."

"I may have to buy a third cookie jar if this keeps up," she said with a laugh. "What type of cookies are we baking today?"

"I thought I'd do something fun and seasonal. My plan was voodoo doll gingerbread men. I've made the icing already. What do you think?"

"That sounds great," Lilah said. "I bet people will love them. What should I do?"

"You can be on beater duty again if you want. I've already got the butter out; it should be soft enough by now. If you want to grab the beater and a mixing bowl out of the cupboard, I'll measure out the brown sugar. Get a big bowl; we're going to be making a double batch."

Once the softened butter and brown sugar had been mixed together, Margie spooned in a few dollops of molasses and a couple of eggs while Lilah continued to man the beater. After that came the dry ingredients and the spices, and in no time at all, they had a bowl full of brown cookie dough that smelled strongly of nutmeg and ginger.

"We'll chill it for a little bit, then roll it out and cut shapes," her friend said. "In the meantime, I thought we could put up some decorations. I've accumulated quite a few boxes of them over the years, so if you want to take any over to your own house, be my guest."

"Thanks," Lilah said. "I might take you up on that. Maybe it would get me back in the holiday spirit."

"The whole town has been subdued since the murder," Margie said. She gave a sigh. "Poor Mark. And I feel so bad for his wife. They've been managing that farm for years. I can hardly believe that something so horrible happened there."

"I can barely believe it myself, and I saw it. I can't imagine what Mrs. Perry must be going through." Lilah frowned, then shook herself, trying to snap out of the glum mood. She had spent all day the day before moping about her house, too lost in her guilt to do anything productive. "Let's start decorating. I need something else to focus on, something besides death."

She soon realized the irony of her words; the very first item that she pulled out of the closest tote was a foam gravestone. She snorted and tossed it back, reaching instead for a giant spider with bendable legs. Margie pulled a long string of orange and black lantern lights out of a second container and began stringing them up along the top of the cupboards. The two women worked in companionable silence for a good half-hour until the kitchen timer beeped.

"We should be able to roll the dough out pretty well by now," Margie said. "Chilled dough always holds its shape best."

"I know — I found that out the hard way," Lilah sad. "When I made those sugar cookies and tried to roll it out at room temperature — it was a mess."

Her friend chuckled. "It sounds like you've been doing a good amount of experimenting on your own. You probably could have made these gingerbread men by yourself, and I bet they would have turned out just as well as if I made them."

"I doubt it," Lilah said, wrinkling her nose. The memory of her disastrous first attempt at cookie making on her own still stung. She had learned a valuable lesson about why it was important to follow the recipe, and not just throw ingredients into a bowl and hope for the best.

"I'm serious, Lilah," Margie said as she pulled the bowl of chilled dough out of the freezer. "You're good at this. You just need more confidence. You should consider setting up a table at the Granger Farm when they reopen. I used to set one up every year, but I've just been too busy this year to do anything but bring the meringues on opening day. I'm sure they would love to have someone else sell cookies there."

"Really?" Lilah turned the idea over in her mind. She still wasn't completely convinced that she had what it took to make cookies for the public, let alone ask people to pay their hard-earned money for them. On the other hand, she trusted Margie's judgement. The older woman knew her baked goods, that was for sure. Maybe it *was* a good idea. She doubted the corn maze and haunted hayride would reopen any time soon, that is if they reopened at all this year. She could use the extra money, and she had already planned on having all of her evenings be taken up by work at the farm. Even if no one bought any cookies from her, she wouldn't be out more than the cost of the ingredients and whatever the cost of setting up a table was.

"You know what, maybe I'll give it a try," she said.

"Great. I'm glad to hear it," Margie said. "Now, grab a rolling pin and help me cut out these gingerbread men."

Within twenty minutes, the warm kitchen was filled with the scent of baking ginger cookies. The first batch came out of the oven absolutely perfect. Lilah smiled at the sight of the little cookie men lined up on the baking tray. They looked like something she might see in a magazine. Once again, she was surprised by just how easy it was to make them — and how many a single batch of dough could produce. They even tasted better than store-bought cookies, and were probably healthier, though she had never bothered to figure out exactly how many calories were in one of her homemade sugar cookies.

Margie hadn't been exaggerating when she said that she wanted to make a lot of cookies. It was hard work, and it was well into nighttime when they finally finished frosting the last tray. Lilah sat down heavily at the kitchen table, exhausted. She didn't mind, though. At least it took her mind off of Mark's death, and she would probably sleep like a log that night.

"Thanks so much for your help, dear," Margie said. She was puttering around the kitchen, still powered by her seemingly inexhaustible supply of energy. "How many should I pack up for you?"

"Oh, just a few. I really shouldn't be eating so many cookies. Maybe I can stop by the boutique tomorrow after my shift at the diner and give some to Val."

"I'll give you extra, then. From what you've told me, that woman could use some cheering up."

A few minutes later, Lilah walked out the front door with a large container full of cookies in her arms. She knew that she would never be able to eat them all, but was more than happy to have the chance to share them with her friends. The long evening of baking had helped her to feel better — maybe eating the cookies would somehow have a similar effect on her best friend.

CHAPTER NINE

T he farm was finally open for business again, though the haunted corn maze and hayride were still temporarily shut down while the police questioned the rest of the employees. Lilah wasn't sure that it was a good idea to reopen either attraction this year. After all, the killer still hadn't been caught. For all she knew, the person who had killed Mark could still be on the farm somewhere.

Those were her thoughts as she parked Margie's car in the nearly empty lot an hour after her shift at the diner. She looked around, not feeling very encouraged by what she saw. It was a foggy afternoon, with a light, intermittent rain, and as a result, most people had opted to stay indoors for the day rather than visit the farm. Lilah was a firm believer of safety in numbers, and wasn't at all comfortable at the thought of being one the only people on the Granger Farm that day. If the killer was going to strike again, this gloomy day seemed like the perfect setting.

Deciding that it would be best to get in and out as quickly as she could, Lilah hurried the short distance from her car to the overhang at the entrance of the little farm shop and reached for the door. A grimace crossed her face when she saw the sign; *Out for lunch!* She glanced at her phone. It was nearly one. Surely whoever was on staff today would be back by then? She didn't want to leave and come back later; all she had to do was grab her first paycheck. It wouldn't take more than a few seconds. Though, if Mrs. Perry was there, she might broach the subject of setting up a small table to sell some cookies on. She was in love with the idea that she and Margie had discussed a couple of days ago. In fact, she had liked it so much that she had spent her extra time trying out a few more recipes. Now her freezer was stuffed with chocolate chip cookies, apple cider cookies, and even a few different flavors of no-bake cookies. Now all she had to do was secure a table at the farm's market to sell them.

Lilah quickly got tired of standing by the door. She eyed the bench — the same one she had sat on with Reid the day of the murder, in fact — critically, trying to decide if it was worth the wet seat of her pants that she would get if she sat down. She decided it wasn't; she might as well just go and sit in the car, where at least she'd be dry.

Just as she was turning, she heard the wet squelch of footsteps coming from around the corner of the farm shop. She turned, expecting to see Mrs. Perry approaching, but instead saw a woman about her own age that she didn't recognize. It took her a moment to realize that the woman was crying — at first she mistook the tears for rain, but the woman's red-rimmed eyes and her shuddering breaths soon made it clear that she was suffering.

"Are you okay?" Lilah asked hesitantly, not certain whether the proper course of action was to try to console the woman, or offer her a shoulder to cry on.

"I'm just —" the woman sniffed. "Just reliving memories. I'm sorry. I know I'm a mess. I thought today would be a good day to visit. The rain, you know, I didn't think anybody would be here."

"I wouldn't be here if I didn't have to pick up my check," Lilah told her. "It really is a pretty terrible day to be wandering around the farm." She felt awkward, and at a loss for words. What in the world was there to be said to this crying stranger?

"Yeah." The woman sniffed again, then gave a small laugh. "I guess it was pretty dumb of me to come out here like this, huh? Now, not only am I crying, but I'm soaked through with rain, and I have to use the bathroom, but there aren't any other guests so that horrible Mrs. Perry is sure to notice me when I go inside. And the *last* thing that I want is to run into her."

Lilah blinked, certain that she had heard the woman wrong. Mrs. Perry had never been anything but pleasant to her, and she couldn't imagine the older woman even raising her voice at anybody.

"Wait a second," the woman said suddenly. "Did you say you work here?"

"I started a couple of weeks ago," Lilah told her, glad for the change in subject. "I'm just here seasonally, so I don't have a key or anything, sorry."

The woman followed her gaze to the locked shop door. "Oh, no, I was actually wondering for a different reason. I'm Gabrielle Ackers, Gabby if you'd like. I'm… I was a friend of Mark's. I was wondering if you were there. You know, the night that he died."

"Lilah Fallon. Nice to meet you," she said automatically. "And yeah, I was there." She didn't say anything more, hoping the woman would let it drop.

"Did you... see anything?" Gabby asked.

Lilah hesitated. She really didn't want to talk about that night again, not with this woman. Even worse than reliving the moments of the murder was the terrible guilt that welled up inside her whenever she thought of the way that she had frozen seconds before Mark had been killed. She didn't want to admit to this stranger that she had been such a coward.

"Please?" the woman said softly. "I need to know. I need to hear it from someone who isn't a cop."

"I saw it," Lilah said, her voice quiet. She hoped that Gabby would get the message and not ask her anything more.

"Do you have any idea who was in the mummy costume? Please, it's important to me." The other woman's eyes were wide and sincere, and Lilah relented a bit, realizing that this was probably even harder for Gabby, who had known Mark personally.

"I'm sorry, but I honestly don't know. According to my friend, both of the mummies were last-minute substitutions. Mark was the one that made the arrangements, and I think if anyone else knew, they would have come forward by now. Everything happened so fast that night. It was dark, and I was on the other side of the path, in the orchard. Even if the person hadn't been wearing a costume, chances are I wouldn't have been able to identify them."

"I understand," Gabby said. Her eyes were brimming with tears again. "Thank you, Lilah. I think I'm going to head home now. I'm sorry for pressing you for answers like that. I don't know if you've ever lost someone close to you, but all I can think about is what I could have done differently."

Lilah understood. She watched sadly as the woman walked away, considering the emotionally draining conversation that she had just had. Gabby hadn't come out and said it, but she had the sneaking suspicion that the woman had been more than just Mark's friend. It would explain her dislike for Mrs. Perry, and how emotional she had been at the thought of the farm manager's death. That raised a new question. If Mark Perry had been having an affair, did that make his wife a possible suspect in his murder?

Lilah jumped at the sound of a key in the door behind her and forced the thought out of her head. Mrs. Perry was back from lunch, which meant it was time for her to pick up her paycheck, and ask about how to rent a table in the shop's small market area to sell cookies. Despite everything that Gabby had said, her gut told her that Mrs. Perry was just as she seemed; a sweet farmer's wife who would never lift a hand against anybody.

CHAPTER TEN

"Here you go. A double bacon burger with two slices of avocado, an egg over easy, and waffle fries on the side. Do you need anything else?" Lilah asked as she set the plate down in front of the burly trucker.

"Not right now. Looks good. Thanks."

"I'll be by in a few minutes to see how you're doing."

Trying not to think of how delicious that burger looked, she pushed back through the swinging doors to the kitchen and threw herself into a chair, looking hopefully at the clock. Forty-five minutes to go until her shift was over and she could get some lunch and go home. Today would be her first day running the little booth that she was renting from Mrs. Perry, and she couldn't wait to set it up. Margie had stopped in earlier, and the two of them had spent a long time talking about logistics; how many cookies she should bring, how to store them, and what sort of allergy information she was likely to be asked about. She hadn't realized that there was much more to selling cookies than just making them and setting them out on a plate, but none of it seemed too difficult to grasp.

It was a slow day at the diner, and time seemed to be inching by at half speed. So few customers meant that she spent most of her time trying to look busy while not making any tips, and trying to stay out of Randall's way while he fiddled with one of the many ancient appliances in the kitchen that seemed to be constantly breaking. She preferred the busy days, when the tips just came rolling in and time flew by. Anything beat twiddling her thumbs, so she grabbed a mop and decided to tackle the kitchen floor, which saw more than its fair share of spilled food and drinks every day. The area by the deep fryer was especially bad, but Randall was currently shoulders deep in the cupboard beneath the fryer, so she'd have to save that spot for later.

Humming to herself and surreptitiously turning the volume up on the radio that was constantly playing in the kitchen, Lilah began to mop, swishing clean, soapy water across the floor, then scrubbing with the mop for a few moments before wringing it out and repeating the process. It was easy to lose herself in the music, and it wasn't until she heard the jingle of the diner's front door open that she remembered her single customer with a start.

Putting down the mop, she pushed through the kitchen doors, relieved to see that the man with the avocado burger seemed to be engrossed in his phone, and still had half a plate of food left and plenty of drink. She turned to the newcomer and was opening her mouth to tell him to sit wherever he wanted when she realized that the man standing by the register was Reid.

"I thought you might be working today," he said, giving her his crooked smile.

"I work pretty much every day," she pointed out. "What can I get you? I think the deep fryer's down. Randall's been working on it for about twenty minutes now."

"That's fine," Reid said. "I think I'll just get chicken club. Two of them, actually."

"Coffee?"

"Just water, please."

"All right. It'll be just a minute. Sit wherever you'd like. It's not exactly busy today."

A few minutes later, she brought out his club sandwiches and a cup of ice water, pausing on her way to his table to drop off the other customer's bill. When she got to Reid's table and delivered his sandwiches, he surprised her by sliding one of them to the other side of the table.

"It's for you," he said.

"What?"

"It's slow in here, and I'm sure you're hungry."

"How did you…? Oh." Lilah sighed. "Margie."

Reid had grown up in the house next to the older woman — the very house that Lilah lived in now, in fact — and she seemed to think of him as something of a son. She had long suspected that Margie was trying to set them up, and that Reid was an active participant in some of her plots. Her friend must have called Reid after she had seen how slow the diner was that day. Come to think of it, Lilah was pretty sure that she had complained to her about skipping breakfast when she had come in earlier. The older woman could be sneaky, that was certain.

Now she was trapped. She could be rude and go back into the kitchen and mop a stretch of floor that really didn't need it while her stomach growled, or she could sit down and eat with him and likely get drawn into yet another awkward conversation.

The club sandwich *did* look pretty good.

"Thanks," she said grudgingly, taking the seat across from him.

"How's everything going?"

"The same as always," he said with a shrug as he salted his sandwich. "Greg Motts — remember him? — turned in his two weeks' notice the other day. I guess he's actually going to open that toy shop he always kept talking about."

"That's great," Lilah said, smiling. "I'm glad things are starting to look up for him." She meant it. Poor Greg had lost both his girlfriend and his mother in the span of a few short weeks a little while ago. With one of the women in his life dead, and the other in prison, things hadn't exactly been going well for him. It sounded like he was beginning to thrive now that he was on his own and had had some time to adjust to his losses.

"I hope he's successful. It's not always easy to start a new business, especially not in a town as small as Vista," Reid said. "Anyway, how have you been holding up?"

She knew immediately that he was talking about the murder. She bit back a sigh. As predicted, he chose the one subject that she most wanted to forget about. "I don't like thinking about it," she said honestly. "I feel terrible, like it was all my fault."

"Me, too," he said, surprising her.

"How would it be *your* fault?" she asked, puzzled.

"Well, I helped get a lot of those signatures, too," he said. "If we hadn't fought so hard to keep the hayride open, then Mark Perry would have gone through with that deal. He wouldn't have rescinded."

Lilah blinked, completely lost for a few seconds. When she realized what he was talking about, her eyes went wide. "You think it was that Don guy that killed him?"

"Don't you?"

"I hadn't really thought about it," she admitted. "I mean, I did think it could have been him fleetingly, but I was too worried about Val right after it happened to give it much thought." And then she had been too busy wallowing in her own sense of guilt to try to figure out who had killed him, but there was no way that she was going to admit *that* to Reid.

"Well, I think it makes the most sense. We heard that argument just hours before Perry was killed."

"That's true. Have you told anyone about it?"

"I gave a statement to the police," he said. "It seemed like the right thing to do. From what we heard, Don definitely had a motive to kill the farm manager."

Lilah nodded, but she wasn't completely convinced. Did it really make sense to murder someone who owed you money? A dead man wouldn't be paying back any debts, and from what she had heard, Don really wanted that money back.

CHAPTER ELEVEN

Lilah drank a cold cup of coffee as quickly as she could at her kitchen table while Winnie looked on imploringly. When she was finished, she reached into the owl jar and tossed a treat to the dog, then retreated to the bathroom for a quick shower to wash the fried food smell off of herself before heading over to the Granger farm. She'd accidentally stayed longer than she had to at the diner. She had been so involved in her conversation with Reid about who the killer was that the end of her shift had come and gone without her even noticing.

The last thing that she wanted was to be late setting up her own table. The cookies that she had made over the last few days were in neatly labeled bags in her freezer, and she had a farm style tablecloth that she had borrowed from Val folded up and ready to go on the counter. Margie would be bringing her metal lock box when she came to pick Lilah up, so she would have somewhere to put the cash that she would hopefully be making from her sales, and she had even thought ahead far enough to buy a package of small paper lunch bags so people would have something to carry their cookies home in. She wasn't necessarily expecting to make a lot of sales this first day, but she had her hopes that she would get a good number of repeat customers over the next few days. Even if she never sold more than a few cookies, at least she would be putting smiles on a few faces. The farm needed something to lift people's spirits after all that had happened this season.

"Thanks so much for helping me, Margie."

"After all you've done for me, don't even mention it," her friend said. The older woman put her hands on her hips and looked at the car. "You're positive we have everything?"

"Yep, we've got it all," Lilah said. "A tablecloth, the lock box, paper bags, platters, hand sanitizer, and enough cookies to feed an army."

"Let's get going, then. I'm eager to get you set up. I think your cookies are going to be quite the hit."

With the two main attractions still shut down, the farm wasn't nearly as busy as it normally was on such a nice day. The parking lot wasn't even half full, and there were only a couple of customers in the line for cider and donuts inside the small farm shop. Mrs. Perry smiled and waved at Lilah as she and Margie walked in. Lilah returned the wave, but her smile was only half-hearted. Ever since meeting Gabby, who she suspected had been having an affair with Mark, she had been unable to shake the nagging thought that Mrs. Perry could be the killer. Her conversation with Reid earlier hadn't done anything to help that. While he was convinced that Don had done it, she thought that Mark Perry's wife had a better motive. Nothing was more dangerous than a woman scorned.

Margie stuck around just long enough to help her set up the table, then she had to go to one of the various clubs that she attended in town. Lilah felt self-conscious sitting alone at her little table, filled with doubts about whether she should be doing this. Why had she thought that her cookies were good enough to sell? She hadn't been baking that long. All she had done was follow some recipes, and try to add a unique flair of her own to the cookies when she could. She hadn't done anything that the average person with too much free time on their hands and a basic ability to follow directions couldn't do.

Lilah forced her concerns down as her first potential customer approached. The woman, her two children in tow, peered at the selection of cookies.

"Are they all homemade?" she asked.

"Yes, I made them all myself," Lilah said.

"The no-bakes look good. Can I have a chocolate one? Kids, you can each pick out a cookie, too."

Lilah packed up the chocolate no-bake cookie, a regular chocolate chip cookie, and a dyed orange sugar cookie frosted to look like a Jack o' lantern. She handed over the bag and took the lady's money, then watched the family walk away, stunned at how easy her first sale had been.

She made another couple of sales in the next hour, but what really made her day was when one of her customers came back a few minutes after buying his first cookie and told her how good they were, then bought three more to take home to his wife and kids. She no longer felt foolish for thinking that she could sell her cookies; instead, she found herself planning out what to try making next. There was a whole world of cookies out there, and the possibilities seemed endless.

Her good mood lasted nearly until closing time, when someone that she recognized walked into the little farm shop. Don, the man who had gotten so angry at Mark for rescinding the sale of the haunted hayride props, ignored her cookie table completely and walked straight up to the register, where Mrs. Perry was seated. The widow sat up straighter as he approached.

"It's been long enough," Lilah heard him say. He made no effort to lower his voice. "I gave you some time after your husbands passing, as is proper, but he and I had a deal. He owed me money, and that doesn't change just because he ain't around anymore. I need that cash."

"Like I said before, Mr. Hinkle, I'll be happy to get you your deposit back just as soon as you show me your receipt," the older woman said.

"And I told you I lost the receipt. My youngest daughter got a hold of it. You know how kids are."

"I'm sorry, and I know it must be frustrating, but I can't just hand over a couple hundred dollars without any proof that that's the amount that my husband owed you," she told him.

"What are you tellin' me? That I'm not going to get that money back?" Don leaned over the register threateningly, but Mrs. Perry kept a straight back and stared him down.

"I'm happy to refund you whatever amount you can prove was owed to you, Mr. Hinkle," she said with a note of finality in her voice. "That is my final answer."

Don glared daggers, but he seemed to know that there was nothing he could do. Mrs. Perry had an air of confidence that even her husband had been lacking, and Lilah got the feeling that she would be a hard person to bully.

"I'll be back," the man said at last.

"Good, we love return customers." She smiled sweetly at him. Without another word, he turned around and slammed his way through the door. Mrs. Perry seemed to deflate as she glanced over at Lilah.

"I'm sorry about that," she said. "He's been bothering me on and off for days. I don't think I'm being unfair, do you?"

"No," Lilah said. "Well, I mean, I completely understand your point of view. But he *did* make that deal with Mr. Perry."

The older woman raised her eyebrows. "How do you know that?"

"I overheard it while I was in the corn maze on my first day," she admitted.

"Hmm. That might change things," Mrs. Perry said, looking out through the glass window in the door through which Don Hinkle had just left. "If he's not trying to pull the wool over my eyes, then maybe I should just give him the money."

Wishing deeply that she had just stayed out of it, Lilah turned her attention to reorganizing the display on her cookie table. She didn't particularly like Don, but she wasn't sure that she completely trusted Mrs. Perry, either. She definitely didn't want to get in the middle of a money feud between them. Either one could be the killer, and Lilah had never been a fan of fifty-fifty odds.

CHAPTER TWELVE

"It's chilly out tonight," Val said, pulling her witch's hat down tightly on her head. "It's that breeze, combined with the humidity from the fog machines. It makes it clammy."

"I don't think it's that bad. It's better than roasting under the sun," Lilah said.

"Well, that's because you're covered from shoulder to toe in burlap and straw," her friend said. "You're wearing a quality costume. This witch dress is thin. And the makeup makes my face feel weird."

The scarecrow eyed her friend's green face paint and grinned. "Playing the part of a witch suits you pretty well, Val. You look good in green."

"Oh, hush. I only volunteered because I didn't want you to have to be alone out here, you know."

"I know. Thanks," Lilah said more solemnly. "I really do appreciate it."

The owners of the Granger Farm had finally managed to get around enough of the legal loopholes and bad press to get the corn maze and hayride running again. Those were the two big money-makers for the season, and Lilah supposed they couldn't stay shut down forever. Still, she had felt a cold dread seep into her bones when she got the call from Mrs. Perry asking her to come back to work as a scarecrow. The killer was still out there, and she didn't necessarily feel that the farm's new no-mask rule did much to keep them safe. Besides, she had been reluctant to close her little cookie stand down. It had been doing so well the past few days. Still, she had made a commitment when she took the job at the farm, it didn't feel right to back out now, not when she knew that so many of the other employees had already left. Besides, playing the part of a scarecrow paid better than her little cookie stand did, and her new resolution to try to make a business out of cookies made her even more eager to make some extra cash when she could.

"I'm not sure why the owners thought this was a good idea," Val said, shifting on her feet and peering down the path as she waited for the tractor and trailer to appear. "Who's even going to show up to a haunted hayride where someone died a week ago?"

"I'm sure plenty of people will show up," Lilah said. "Probably not as many families with kids. But it's Halloween. People want to be scared. There will probably be a lot of teens, hoping to see a glimpse of real blood."

"Maybe some real life ghost hunters, too," Val said. She pursed her lips, eying the dark stretch of forest across from them where Mark had breathed his last. "Do you believe in ghosts, Lilah? Real ones, not women walking around in sheer dresses stained with fake blood."

"I'm not sure. I've never seen one, but my father's office building used to have this one meeting room in which the door kept opening for no reason that anybody could find. I was there alone one night, working late, and I heard it creak open down the hall. It was the creepiest thing that has ever happened to me. We always latched that door, there was no reason it would have opened like that."

"What did you do?" her friend asked.

"I called the building janitor up to have him look at it, then followed him downstairs and left. I never stayed at the office alone at night after that," Lilah said. She shivered as she relived the memory, feeling the horror that she had felt all those years ago when she had heard that slow creak coming from behind her in a building that she knew to be empty.

"Ugh, maybe telling horror stories isn't a good idea right now," Val said with a shudder. "Even if ghosts aren't real, Mark's killer is still on the loose, and we have no idea who it is."

"Actually," Lilah said. "I do have an idea of who may have done it." She told her friend about her run-in with Gabby and her theory that Mark Perry had been having an affair. To her surprise, Val nodded sagely when she was done.

"Oh, everybody knows that," her friend said. "I've been volunteering here for years, remember? Anyone who has worked here for long enough would have stumbled across them at some point. Even his wife knew. From what I've heard, she was on the verge of divorcing him, but wanted to keep their public image good for the business. Everyone in town likes to think of them as the sweet couple that runs the Granger Farm. A separation would wreck that image."

"Well then, what do you think about Mrs. Perry as a murder suspect?" Lilah asked.

Val snorted. "I don't see it. I mean, maybe when she first found out years ago, but this has been going on for so long... why would she snap now? They've been acting more like business partners than husband and wife lately. I think she's past the point of caring. Besides, that mummy moved pretty well, and Mrs. Perry has arthritis in her knees. She wouldn't have been able to run away so fast after she did it."

"I suppose you're right. Come to think of it, she's shorter than you, isn't she? And you said the mummy was a little bit taller."

Her friend nodded. "You're right." She frowned slightly, considering. "But, now that you mention it, Mark's girlfriend's pretty tall, isn't she? I've never spoken to her, but I've seen her around a few times."

"She's tall," Lilah said, "but I don't see why she would kill him. She seemed really upset about losing him, and she kept asking me if I knew who the killer was, or if I recognized anything about the mummy."

"Well, Mark's been visiting with her on the side for years, hasn't he?" Val asked. "Maybe she didn't like the fact that after all that time, he was still with his wife. Or maybe he tried to break it off with her, who knows. Johnny said that he heard them arguing a while back, but I don't remember about what. I never liked Mark very much, but I wish I had paid more attention now."

"Maybe she was asking me if I had any idea who the mummy was to see if I recognized her," Lilah said, beginning to see that Gabby made a pretty good suspect. "Oh my goodness, Val, do you think she would have killed me if I'd said the wrong thing? Maybe she was there that afternoon to cover her tracks."

"It could be," her friend said. "I mean, anyone who's willing to have an affair with someone else's spouse can't be a very good person, can they? Hold on — I think the tractor's coming."

The two women took a break from their conversation and hid in the shadows. As the trailer passed, Lilah did her usual routine, staggering out of the shadows and reaching for the people on the trailer, while Val ran out in front of it, cackling in a very witch-like way.

"It was definitely an older crowd tonight," her friend said after the trailer had passed out of sight. "No one wants to bring their kids to a murder scene."

"I don't blame them," Lilah said. "But listen, there's another suspect. Reid and I were talking about this the other day. I don't think I ever told you, but I overheard Mark and this guy named Don talking…"

Val listened while she relayed the story, a frown appearing on her face that only deepened as Lilah got further in. She ended with the last time she had seen him, and the encounter between him and Mrs. Perry.

"Now that's something you should be telling to the police," her friend said. "Are you the only one that overheard those conversations?"

"Reid was with me when Don and Mark were arguing for the last time," Lilah said. "The first time I heard them speaking, I was the only one there. Then when Don came to collect his deposit, it was just me and Mrs. Perry."

"Then the police may not know about this guy at all," Val pointed out. "He sounds like he's an angry person, and potentially dangerous. I mean, who threatens a woman for money just a week after her husband's death?"

"To be fair, Mrs. Perry hasn't exactly been too broken up about losing him." Something occurred to her. "Val, you said the Perry's were considering a divorce, right?"

"It's what I picked up on, but I never spoke to either of them about it directly. I didn't think it was my business to get involved in their relationship."

"I know you said you don't think Mrs. Perry could have killed him, but what if she was going to lose this job at the farm, or lose their house? Maybe she killed him before the divorce so she wouldn't be cut off from whatever benefits they get as a married couple."

"I'm not saying it isn't a motive, but I still don't think she could have physically done it." Val sighed. "This conversation hasn't been exactly comforting. I started off the evening having no idea who the killer might be. The fact that there's three suspects doesn't exactly make me feel much better. And where is that next tractor, anyway? It's been way too long."

As she spoke, Lilah's radio crackled to life. It was Johnny, telling them that the farm was closing early and they were free to go home — not enough people had shown up for the haunted hayride for them to be able to keep running it that night.

"After all we went through to save it, and it's just getting shut down anyway," Lilah said with a sigh. "Come on, let's go. I think you're right — I do need to tell the police what I know about Don. I can swing by the station on my way home."

CHAPTER THIRTEEN

A n hour after Lilah got home that night, her cell phone rang. At first she was reluctant to answer it, certain that whoever it was couldn't have good news, not after a day as stressful and depressing as the one that she had just had. Still, she dragged herself off of the couch and over to the kitchen counter where she had left her purse, and was glad that she did when she saw who was calling. It was Margie, and what her neighbor said over the phone warmed her right up.

"Thanks for inviting me over for dinner, Margie," Lilah said after making the short walk over to the older woman's house. "It's been a crazy couple of weeks. I could use the company."

"Well, I figured you might be a bit down when I saw you come home from work so early. I got a wonderful deal on Cornish game hens from the butcher today, and my first thought was to make something nice to celebrate your success with your cookies. I was going to do it tomorrow night, but tonight will work just as well."

"It's been a pretty bad evening," Lilah admitted. "The haunted hayride got closed down after only one group of people went through. I guess no one wanted to take the chance that they would be the next victim. I don't think they're going to bother reopening it again until the killer is caught. And to make matters worse, I stopped at the police station on the way home to tell the officer in charge of the investigation about a couple of suspects that Val and I were discussing, and he pretty much just told me that the police had already questioned the people that I mentioned, and that they were perfectly capable of doing their job without my help." She sighed. "He told me that it was dangerous for everyone involved when civilians got mixed up in police work, and basically said that I should keep my nose out of it."

"Oh, don't pay any mind to him. His dad was the old chief of police, and he's very sensitive to people telling him how to do his job. He thinks it means he's not good enough, I'm guessing. Come on into the kitchen, and I'll put the finishing touches on dinner."

Lilah followed her friend into her kitchen and helped her prepare the mashed potatoes as they continued talking. "Maybe I'll be able to keep selling cookies in the farm store, now that Johnny's saying they probably won't run the haunted hayride again this season. That will give some time to sell extra cookies, at least."

"I think that's a good idea. From what Val said, those cookies of yours are quite the hit."

"Did she call you?"

"She did. She thought you were selling cookies for me, so she called to congratulate me. She said the cookies were more popular than ever." Her friend chuckled. "She was quite surprised when I told her that you made each and every cookie on your own."

"Well, considering that the only experience she has with my cooking was microwaved instant noodles back when we were in college, I don't blame her. Honestly, I was surprised by how much people seemed to enjoy the cookies, too. I was expecting *some* success — I knew they tasted good, since I sampled every batch myself — but I didn't expect so many repeat customers."

"You have a gift," Margie said simply.

"Too bad I'm only now discovering it," Lilah said, sighing. "I could have spent the last ten years building up a cookie business, instead of wasting time at a job I didn't enjoy."

"It's not too late," her friend said. "Don't start acting like you're too old to do anything useful with your life. Look at me; I'm nearly twice your age, and I still accomplish plenty. I don't follow along with that 'too old' nonsense."

"It's different for you. You're…" she gestured helplessly, at a loss for the right words to describe her neighbor. "You're Margie. Everyone in town knows you. I think you've *helped* everyone in town at least once. People know they can depend on you. But I've only been here for a couple of years, and I haven't exactly got a great reputation. I haven't held on to any job for more than a few weeks since I quit at my father's company. I haven't built *anything* with my life, Margie."

"You're trying to follow your dreams and do what makes you happy," her friend said. "Very few people are brave enough to do that. If you like making cookies, and you're good at it — which you are — I think you should stick with it and make something for yourself out of it."

"What do you mean?"

"Well, you could open a shop," Margie said. She spooned the mashed potatoes into glass bowl, then added, "It's something that I've always wanted to do."

"Why don't you? I think that would be great. Everyone in town already loves your cookies. You'd hardly even have to advertise."

"Oh, I don't have the time or energy for something like that anymore. I've looked into it just enough to know that starting up a new business like that would take up a lot of my time. I enjoy doing all of the things I do now, and running a business would take time away from my other interests. But I think that it would be an amazing idea for you."

"A lot of small businesses fail in the first year," Lilah said as they sat down at the table. "I think almost half of them. I don't know if a cookie shop in such a small town would ever be successful enough to be anything other than a hobby. Plus, where would I get the money for something like that?" She liked the idea; it would be amazing to spend her days baking instead of working in the diner's greasy kitchen. She would be her own boss, she could set her own hours and she certainly knew how to run a business… Lilah shook her head, trying not to get ahead of herself. Even if it was possible for a cookie store to be profitable in a town like Vista, Alabama, she just didn't have the money for start-up costs.

"I think it would be more successful than you'd expect. Vista may be a small town, but there are quite a few other small towns within easy driving distance. And people drive through here all the time on their way to the coast. As for money, well, I've got some saved up." Margie looked at her consideringly. "If you're serious about baking, and think you might want to give this a try, I'd be happy to loan you the money if you come up with a good business plan."

Lilah gaped at her friend. "I couldn't ask you to do that. It's too risky, what if the business failed? You know I don't exactly have the best track record when it comes to jobs. Val says I'm cursed."

Margie chuckled. "I may be old, but that doesn't mean I'm superstitious. I don't believe in curses. And you aren't asking me for the loan. I'm offering. There isn't enough good in this world, and I think a cookie store run by someone as kind-hearted as you are would bring smiles to a lot of faces."

Lilah spent the rest of dinner turning her friend's proposition over in her mind. The prospect of having her very own store was tempting. Val ran her little boutique and seemed to do well enough. In fact, there were a lot of small businesses in town. It was certainly possible to keep a business afloat here. Without the issue of money, what was standing in her way? Nothing. Still, it didn't feel like a decision that she should make without some serious thought. It would be a risky move for both her and Margie if she went through with it.

Feeling conflicted, she thanked her friend for the delicious meal and helped clean up the dishes before going back to her own house. She fed the dog and the cat and put a load of laundry in the washing machine, lost in thought the entire time. She was in the middle of a fantasy about running a thriving cookie store when her phone rang, making her jump. It was late, and once again she worried that the caller bore bad news. She glanced at the caller ID. Val.

"Hello?"

"Lilah, you have to get to the Granger Farm immediately. I was finishing up putting away some of the props, and saw Gabby pull into the lot and get out of her car. She was carrying something in her arms, I don't know what, but whatever she's doing here this late can't be good. I tried calling Mrs. Perry's home number, but she didn't answer, and she's not in the shop. She must be on the farm somewhere. What if Gabby's here to kill her? We have to do *something.* I can't leave without at least warning Mrs. Perry, but I'm terrified to go wandering around the farm on my own looking for her."

Reluctantly, Lilah agreed to head over, more about loyalty to her friend than concern that Gabby was the killer. The woman just hadn't seemed dangerous to her, and the more she thought about it, the more certain she was that Don must have murdered Mark. Still, Val was her best friend, and she couldn't just leave her hanging.

"I'll see if I can borrow Margie's car again. I'll be there soon."

CHAPTER FOURTEEN

L ilah pulled into the Granger Farm parking lot with the headlights on Margie's car switched off. It was a dark night, with clouds covering the stars and a new moon, and she was relatively certain that no one watching from the farmhouse across the clearing would be able to see her. She didn't spot Val's car until she got out and began walking towards the farm shop. Her friend was parked in the darkest, most shadowy corner of the lot, under the low-hanging bough of a stand of trees.

Feeling uneasy, Lilah approached the farm shop and hissed her friend's name. Val hadn't mentioned where exactly she was on the farm, and Lilah hadn't thought to ask. She hoped her friend didn't expect her to go wandering off into the cornfield or orchard alone, looking for her, because that was definitely not going to happen.

"Val," she called again, a little bit louder. "Where *are* you?"

A shadowy form came around the corner of the farm shop, and Lilah jumped.

"Relax, it's just me," her friend said in a low voice. "You got here sooner than I thought you would, sorry. I followed Gabby back towards the big barn, but I didn't want to go further alone. I'm not sure what she's doing here, but it can't be good."

Lilah agreed with that assessment. The two women being near each other wouldn't lead to anything good. Lilah desperately wanted to prevent the killer from taking another life. She just wished she knew whose life she was supposed to be saving.

"Do you have your phone?" she asked Val. Her friend nodded. "Good. At the first sign of something being not quite right, we'll call the police. I don't think Eldridge will pay any attention to me unless there's some sort of solid evidence that one of these people is the killer. He, ah, didn't take me too seriously when I tried to talk to him earlier today."

"Are you sure you want to do this?" the other woman asked. "I know I'm the one that called you, but now that we're here it doesn't seem like such a good idea. I mean, it's almost pitch black. We can't use any lights or we'll be seen. And what are we going to do if one of them has a gun?"

"Do you want to leave and go home?" Lilah asked hopefully.

Val bit her lip, then shook her head. "No. If someone gets attacked after we leave, I would never forgive myself."

The answer didn't surprise Lilah; when it came down to it, she felt the same way. Both she and Val had witnessed the murder and had done nothing to stop it. Somehow it felt like if they could stop a second murder, it might make up for their lack of action during the first one.

"You said she headed towards the big barn? Let's go that way first. Just keep your eyes peeled. If I get murdered tonight because you called me here, I'm going to haunt you forever."

The farm, which had become so familiar to her in the day, was eerie at night. The buildings created deep shadows, areas of darkness even more intense than the normal darkness of a moonless night. The wind whispered through the dry stalks of corn, a sound that would have made the perfect backdrop to a horror movie. The lowing of a cow almost made Lilah jump out of her skin; it had sounded almost exactly like the moan of someone dressed up in a mummy costume.

"I can see why this place is so popular around Halloween," she whispered to her friend as they walked. "It's creepy even without the props."

Before long, the big barn loomed in front of them. It was the largest building on the property, and didn't house animals, but rather farm equipment. The two women edged closer cautiously, being as quiet as possible as they strained for any sound or hint of light from under the huge sliding barn doors. Nothing.

"If someone's in there, they're sitting in the dark," Val whispered. "What should we do?"

"Are you sure Gabby was coming this way?"

"This was the direction she was heading in," her friend said. "But I didn't follow her very far."

"What's Mrs. Perry's schedule like after the farm closes for the evening?"

"She usually goes around and makes sure everything is locked up. Then, I don't know what. She could be anywhere."

Lilah sighed. This was a lot harder than she had thought it would be. If only they could find Gabby.

"Maybe," she said, "she isn't here to kill anyone and we were just being paranoid. What if she's here to pay her respects to Mark somehow? What was she carrying?"

"I didn't see it clearly. It could have been anything. It was sort of long, covered in white paper, and she was carrying it with one arm.

It could have been a weapon, or something as simple as a bottle of wine."

"Or flowers?" Lilah asked.

"I suppose. But why — oh." Val winced, looking embarrassed.

"You think she might be bringing flowers for Mark?"

"She *did* seem to be really upset about his death when I spoke with her. And if everyone knows that she was his mistress, she may not be welcome on the farm during daylight hours."

"Well, where would she be bringing the flowers? If that's all she's doing, we can leave, but I don't want to chance leaving until we're certain."

"I don't know. Maybe they had a special place where they met... or maybe she's bringing them to the spot where he was killed."

It was the best idea that they had, so Lilah and Val turned away from the barn and began walking towards the cornfield, where the haunted hayride's path began. They would be more visible walking along it than if they went through the orchard, but neither of them wanted to try to find their way through the trees in the dark. A moment later, a piercing scream echoed across the farm. The two women froze and exchanged a glance.

"Hurry!" Lilah said. They began running, but soon had to slow down to pick their way through the dark. One of them getting hurt wouldn't help anybody. It seemed to take forever for them to reach the head of the path, but at last it came into view.

Lilah led the way, but she had only taken a few steps along the dirt path before a noise made her jump. She and Val whirled around, and Val let out a short scream at the sight of the man standing just a few feet away. It was too dark to make out his face, and her first crazy thought was that it was Mark's ghost.

"What are you doing here?" he asked, and she felt a rush of relief when she realized that she knew that voice.

"Johnny, thank goodness, you almost gave me a heart attack," she said. "What are *you* doing here?"

"I saw a girl walk by. I was following her. People aren't supposed to come onto the farm at night. It's dangerous."

"Yeah, we were following her, too. We heard someone scream," Lilah said. "Do you know where she went?"

"I scared her and she ran away. I lost her," he said. "You should leave, too."

With that, he turned and began walking back towards the entrance. Val and Lilah exchanged a glance, then followed him. It looked like their nighttime investigation was over. It hadn't come to any satisfactory conclusion, but at least neither of them had been attacked by a crazed killer.

CHAPTER FIFTEEN

"So who do *you* think killed Mr. Perry?" Lilah asked Johnny, struggling to keep up with his fast pace. "I mean, you've been here a while, right? You must have some idea."

"Lilah," Val said. She was a few feet behind, and falling further back. Realizing with a start that her friend was limping, Lilah stopped walking and hurried back towards her.

"Oh my goodness, what happened?"

"I twisted my ankle when Johnny surprised us," she said. "I'll be okay, I just can't go as fast. You go on ahead, Johnny. We'll catch up."

"Here, lean on me," Lilah said to her friend. "Put your arm around my shoulders. You should have said something sooner."

Val leaned heavily on her and concentrated on hobbling forward in silence for a few moments until Johnny had drawn ahead. Then her grip on her friend's arm tightened and she leaned her head closer to Lilah's so she could whisper in her ear.

"Don't stop walking, and don't react at all to what I'm about to say, but Lilah, I think Johnny is the killer."

Her eyes went wide. She waited to respond for a few more moments until Johnny had drawn even further ahead.

"Why do you think that?" she whispered back.

"He's the right height, and he could easily have been the mummy. But besides that, I think I saw blood on his hand back there. He wiped it on his pants as he turned around."

"Blood?" Lilah asked "Why would he have blood... Oh no. Gabby."

Her friend nodded. "Think about it. We heard a scream just minutes before he came out of nowhere and found us."

"But why would he kill her? That doesn't make sense."

"Maybe she was getting too close to the truth," Val whispered. Just then Johnny looked back and noticed that they had fallen quite a ways behind. He waited for them to catch up.

"Everything all right?" he asked. Val nodded.

"It twinges a bit, but I don't think it's serious. A day or two of rest should put me back to normal."

"Good," Johnny said. "Sorry if I scared you. I know Mrs. Perry likes you. You do a lot to help out around the farm every year. I'm glad you're not hurt bad."

Lilah exchanged a glance with her friend. This man didn't seem like a killer. The blood that Val thought she'd seen could just as easily have been mud or oil from one of the tractors. And considering that Johnny had scared her and Val half to death when he found them, she could believe that the scream that they had heard had been nothing more than a startled scream from Gabby when he found her. She couldn't imagine Johnny hurting someone, or plotting out a murder.

They reached the big barn, and Johnny stopped. He pulled open the huge sliding door and stepped inside the building without explanation. Lilah felt Val tense beside her, and even though she had her doubts that he was the killer, she took a couple of cautious steps away from the dark maw of the barn.

Johnny reappeared a moment later holding a manure shovel. Both women flinched back as he held it out towards them.

"Here you go," he said to Val. "You can use it like a crutch. I feel bad that you got hurt."

Val accepted the shovel somewhat warily and used it to prop herself up. She looked surprised. "Thanks."

"Can you two make it to the parking lot on your own? I have to go find the other girl. She's still here somewhere."

"We'll be fine," Lilah told him, forcing a smile. "Thanks for your help."

He left without another word, vanishing quickly back into the darkness in the direction that they had just come. Lilah exchanged a look with her friend.

"What now?" she asked, keeping her voice low in case Johnny was still hanging around somewhere nearby.

"I don't know," Val whispered back. "Should we leave Gabby here alone with him?"

"He doesn't exactly seem dangerous," Lilah said. "I mean, he gave you a shovel. He seemed to feel bad about scaring us. He hasn't done anything threatening at all."

Val opened her mouth to respond, but the words never came out. Instead her eyes went wide and she raised the shovel defensively. "Watch out!" she shouted.

Lilah jumped aside and spun to face her friend had seen. At first she didn't see anything, then she saw what she had taken to be a shadow break off from the other shadows and move towards them. Val tightened her grip on the shovel, prepared to use it to defend them, and Lilah, weaponless, hid shamelessly behind her friend.

"Wait, don't hurt me," a voice called out. It was a woman's, and one that she instantly recognized as Gabby's.

"Val, put down the shovel," she hissed. She reached into her pocket, tired of not being able to see anything, and pulled out her phone. Turning on the flashlight app, she shone it towards the newcomer's face. She gasped. Gabby had blood around her nose and mouth, and her hair was disheveled.

"What happened?" Lilah asked in a low voice. "Did Johnny do that?"

The other woman nodded. "He came out of nowhere and grabbed me. He called me a whole bunch of horrible names and hit me with something."

"How did you get away?" Val asked. She had lowered the shovel, but was still gripping it tightly, and looked suspicious.

"I kicked him where it counts," Gabby said. "Then I ran as fast as I could. I stopped when I heard someone else scream."

"That was me," Lilah's friend said. "He snuck up on us, too. But why would he attack you?" She raised the shovel slightly. "Did you kill Mark?"

"I would never!" the woman gasped. "I loved him. I was bringing flowers for him. I thought that maybe if I put them at the spot where he died, his spirit might somehow sense it, and he'd know I was thinking of him. I have no idea why Johnny attacked me, and I definitely don't want to stick around to find out. Hurry, let's go."

"Wait a second," Lilah said. "Just, hold on. It doesn't make sense that Johnny would just attack you like that. He found us wandering around too, but he led us back to here and gave Val a shovel to use as a crutch since she twisted her ankle. That doesn't seem like the sort of thing a lunatic would do. How do we know we can believe you?"

"What, did I punch myself in the face?" Gabby asked, her voice rising as she lost her temper. "He's always hated me, ever since he found out about me and Mark. He thought that we were betraying Mrs. Perry, and he hated us for it. Now we have to go. He's going to come back. Please, just run. He's dangerous."

"I think we should go," Val said. "Whether or not Johnny's dangerous to us, he obviously hurt Gabby. She needs to go to a doctor, and I don't think it would be a good idea for her to hang around here until Johnny finds her again."

"Okay. You're right," Lilah said. "But we all go in the same car, and as soon as we drop her off at the hospital, we're going to the police, okay?"

"I don't need a hospital. Let's just go straight to the police," Gabby said. "Now let's *go.*"

They hurried back towards the parking lot as quickly as Val's ankle would let them, which wasn't very fast. A couple of times, they thought that they heard a noise off in the darkness somewhere, but they never saw anything. Lilah was still using her phone's flashlight; even though she knew it made them more visible, she couldn't bear the thought of wandering through the darkness again.

The tight knot of fear that had been in her chest for the last few minutes loosened when they finally reached the little farm shop. Their cars were in the parking lot just beyond, and soon enough they would all be driving to safety.

They headed towards her car, which was the closest. Lilah dug in her pocket for Margie's key, and was just about to hit the button to unlock it when Val said, "Wait."

"What?"

"Look," her friend said softly. "Look at the tires."

She looked, and what she saw made her feel sick. All four tires had been slashed.

"Oh my goodness," Gabby breathed. "He's here. He's watching us."

The three women looked wildly around the parking lot, standing back to back. There was no sign of Johnny in the wide open space.

"I'm going to go check the other cars," Lilah whispered. "Gabby, stay here with Val."

Trying hard to be courageous, she tightened her grip on her phone and ran across the lot to Val's car. It took her only a second to spot its four slashed tires. She turned her phone's light to Gabby's vehicle, with the same results. All three of their cars had flat tires. She thought they still might be able to drive them, but probably not very well or quickly.

When Lilah turned to head back to Val and Gabby and deliver the bad news, she saw something that made her heart stop. The clouds had parted just enough to expose a shadowy figure moving along the wall of the farm shop. The two women had their eyes on her; they didn't see the danger.

Lilah opened her mouth to shout, but the same panic that she felt on the night of the murder rose up in her again. She couldn't get any words out. She couldn't breathe. Her friends were going to die because she was useless — no, she wouldn't let that happen.

Forcing her body to listen to her despite the adrenaline that was running through it, she took a deep breath and yelled, *"Watch out! Behind you!"*

Val turned just in time to see Johnny run at her. He had some sort of farming implement in his hand, and was poised to stab her with it. Not missing a beat, Val raised the shovel and swung. It caught him full in the face as he ran towards her, and he fell over like a toppled tree.

Lilah reached them just as Johnny was struggling to get up. Val had hit him with such force that the shovel had been knocked out of her hands, and the pitchfork that Johnny had been carrying had also been knocked away. His face was streaming blood from a broken nose and split lip, but the hit hadn't knocked him out. Gabby was frozen, watching in horror as the scene unfolded in front of her.

Not knowing what else to do, Lilah picked up the shovel and hit him in the shoulder with it. He fell to his side, groaning. She kept a firm grip on the shovel, keenly aware that it was the only weapon that they had between the three of them.

"Don't move," she warned. "Or I'll hit you again."

"You're crazy," he muttered. "You're protecting a bad lady."

"What do you mean?" Lilah glanced over at Gabby, wondering if they had been hoodwinked. Was it possible that she was the killer after all? Had she been the one who had slashed all of their tires? She hated being so unsure.

"She's a bad lady. She hurt Mrs. Perry. She shouldn't have been with a married man," Johnny mumbled. He seemed somewhat incoherent, probably from the blow to his face he had sustained a few moments ago.

"He loved me!" Gabby cut in. "He would have left her for me like he promised if he hadn't been killed."

"I know," Johnny said. "I had to stop him. He was a bad man. He hurt Mrs. Perry too."

Lilah and Val exchanged a look. Had he just confessed to killing the farm manager?

"I'm calling the police," Gabby announced. "They'll figure all of this out. You're going to rot in prison for life if you killed my Mark, Johnny. And you'll deserve every second behind bars."

PATTI BENNING

CHAPTER SIXTEEN

T he next few hours passed in a blur of too-bright lights and faceless people in uniform. Lilah was questioned multiple times, asked to relay her story first to the police, then to the paramedics who showed up to look over Val and Gabby, then by a news crew that had somehow gotten wind of what had happened. She answered what felt like hundreds of questions, but didn't get a chance to ask any of her own. It wasn't until the next day that she got answers when she tuned in to the local news station during breakfast.

Johnny, it turned out, had confessed everything to the police that night. He had killed Mark in a fit of rage after discovering that Mark was planning on leaving Mrs. Perry and taking everything he could with him. The farm manager's wife had helped Johnny out of a tight spot before, and he was fiercely loyal to her.

He swore that he hadn't been trying to kill Gabby that night. He had lost his temper when he saw her, the adulteress, leaving flowers for another woman's husband. It wasn't until he saw that Gabby had found the other two women and had heard them talk about going to the police that he realized he might have made a mistake. He admitted, the news reported, that he was going to kill them all and hide their bodies in the cornfield. He said he liked Val and Lilah, but he was more concerned about going to jail.

It was a chilling story, and Lilah switched off the television as soon as it was over. She had liked Johnny. She had worked with him quite often over the last couple of weeks. It still seemed surreal that he had been the killer all along.

She was washing her breakfast dishes when someone knocked on her front door. Turning the water off and wiping her hands on the dish towel, she went to see who it was. The peephole showed Margie's familiar, comforting face. Nudging Winnie aside with her foot, she opened the door and invited her friend in with a smile.

"It's good to see you. I'm still a bit freaked out by everything that happened last night."

"I don't blame you," the older woman said, giving a delicate shudder. "I can't imagine going through everything you went through. How are you holding up?"

"It's not too bad. It's good knowing he's in jail. I think this is going to be the hardest for Mrs. Perry and Gabby. They both knew Johnny, and he killed a man that they both cared about."

She opened the door wider and invited Margie in, then went back to cleaning the breakfast dishes. "I'm sorry again about your car," she added. "I'll pay for all new tires."

"It wasn't your fault. They should make Johnny pay for it, as far as I'm concerned," her friend said. "Anyway, I didn't come here to talk about all of that. I figured you could use something to distract you, so I thought we'd start making a business plan."

"A business plan?"

"For the cookie shop," Margie said with a smile. "That is, if you still think you might want to do it."

"I'd have to be crazy not to want to make a living making cookies," Lilah said. She finished drying the last dish and sat at the breakfast table next to her friend. "Do you really it could be successful?"

"Why wouldn't it be? Everyone loves cookies, and you'll get plenty of repeat customers. If Greg Motts thinks he can open a toy shop and make a profit, then someone with your inherent gifts and your knowledge of the business world should be able to do the same with cookies."

"There's so much to think about," she said, overwhelmed. "There can't be that many empty buildings zoned for retail in town, and I'll need one with a kitchen area already set up. And then there's finding suppliers for bulk ingredients, marketing, figuring out what sort of licensure I need to sell food… this is going to be a huge project, Margie."

"I'm up to it, if you are," her friend said, her eyes twinkling. "I haven't been so excited about something in years."

"Neither have I," Lilah admitted. She took a deep breath. "All right. Let's do it."

Made in the USA
Middletown, DE
30 September 2018